Behind The Creation Of. . .

MICKEY MOUSE

Bob Italia

Published by Abdo & Daughters, 6535 Cecilia Circle, Edina, Minnesota 55439.

Library bound edition distributed by Rockbottom Books, Pentagon Tower, P.O. Box 36036, Minneapolis, Minnesota 55435.

Printed in the United States.

ISBN: 1-56239-053-8

Library of Congress Card Catalog Number: 91-073048

Cover Photo: Globe Photos
Inside Photos: Pictorial Parade Inc.

Edited by Rosemary Wallner

CONTENTS

The world's most famous cartoon character—
Mickey Mouse!

MICKEY MOUSE

The Number One Mouse

Mickey Mouse is the world's most famous cartoon character. He has appeared in over 130 movies. He has his own television show. He has made many records. He has appeared in hundreds of comic books. And Mickey Mouse Clubs are found in cities everywhere.

What has made Mickey Mouse so popular? Is it his funny stories? Is it his funny looks? Or is it because Mickey was one of the very first cartoon characters? That's what we're going to find out.

Mickey's Two "Fathers"

Almost everyone knows that Walt Disney created Mickey Mouse. But Disney had help from a friend named Ub Iwerks (Eye-werks).

In 1919, 17-year-old Walt Disney met Ub Iwerks in Kansas City, Missouri. Both were artists at Pesmen-Rubin Commercial Art Studio. Eventually, they became good friends.

Disney was not happy working for Pesmen-Rubin. The work he did for them was boring. Disney had recently learned about a new type of motion picture called *animated film* (drawings that move), and he wanted to start his own animation company. In 1922, Disney did just that. He called his company Laugh-o-Gram Films, Inc. His friend Ub Iwerks came to work for Disney.

Disney's company failed in one year. He traveled to Hollywood, California, in search of work. He rented a studio and started making more silent, black-and-white animated films. Disney drew all the characters and scenes. One of his films was titled *Alice's Wonderland*, which Disney sold for $1,500 to Margaret J. Winkler, a New York film distributor. Suddenly, he became so busy that he called Ub Iwerks for help. Once again, Disney and Iwerks were working together.

Disney and Iwerks created a new cartoon character called Oswald the Lucky Rabbit. They thought Oswald would become very popular—and make them very rich.

But there were problems. Disney was still working for Margaret Winkler. Winkler had just married Charles Mintz, who began to run Winkler's business. Mintz was also a business partner with Universal Pictures. So the Oswald character belonged to Universal—not to Disney. Universal Pictures decided to use their own animators to make more Oswald cartoons. Disney was not allowed to draw Oswald—his own creation—again.

Mortimer Mouse?

Disney was crushed. Now he had to start all over again. But he was determined to create another funny character that would please movie audiences.

One night, while on a very long train ride, Disney scribbled as many new characters onto his pad as he could. Finally, he came up with one that excited him—a mouse.

"Look," Disney said to his wife, holding up the sketch, "Mortimer Mouse!"

"Mortimer?" his wife Lillian complained. "Mortimer is a horrible name for a mouse!"

Disney argued with his wife for a while, then came up with a new name—*Mickey Mouse.*

Disney's wife liked that name much better.

Mickey Mouse was Disney's idea. Disney wrote all of Mickey's stories. But the final figure of

Mickey Mouse was created by Ub Iwerks. He came up with the design for Mickey that would be used in all the upcoming cartoons.

Mickey's First Cartoon

Mickey's first black-and-white animated film was called *Plane Crazy.* It was made in 1928, and did not have any sound. (No movies at that time had any sound).

In the cartoon, Mickey builds an airplane for an around-the-world trip with the help of his farm-yard friends . But Mickey's plane crashes before it can leave the barnyard. Mickey rebuilds the plane using parts from his car, then takes his girlfriend, Minnie Mouse, for a ride. (Minnie Mouse was created so Mickey could have some-one to save in this cartoon—and in many more cartoons to come.) *Plane Crazy* was shown at a Hollywood movie-house, and the audience loved it.

Minnie Mouse appeared in Mickey's
first movie, *Plane Crazy.*

Disney decided to make another Mickey Mouse film. The second film was called *Gallopin' Gaucho*, and it was ready by the end of 1928. In this silent film, Mickey saves Minnie from the evil Pegleg Pete in a South American jungle. This cartoon was not as popular as *Plane Crazy*, but Disney went ahead with plans for a third Mickey Mouse cartoon titled *Steamboat Willie.*

Mickey Speaks!

While Disney and his studio worked on their newest cartoon, the first motion picture with sound, *The Jazz Singer*, was released by Warner Brothers Studios. Disney was excited by this new type of film, and decided to make *Steamboat Willie* with sound. Iwerks did most of the drawing, with the help of a new assistant, Les Clark. The voice of Mickey was Walt Disney. *Steamboat Willie* was the first cartoon with sound—and it became an instant hit. No one had ever seen anything like it.

Mickey Mouse as he appeared in
Steamboat Willie.

Not only was *Steamboat Willie* a hit, but Mickey Mouse became an instant star. Realizing this, Disney created a Mickey Mouse comic strip for the newspapers. Disney wrote the stories, and Iwerks did all the drawing.

How They Make Mickey Move

At first, Mickey Mouse was created out of circles. Pennies and dimes were used by the cartoonist to draw the circles. Mickey had black dots for eyes, and very thin arms and legs. Also, he had only three fingers and a thumb on each white-gloved hand. The fingers and thumb in a glove were easy to illustrate and this saved the cartoonist a lot of drawing time. Because the cartoonist didn't have to spend long hours drawing Mickey, Disney saved millions of dollars.

The cartoonist drew on sheets of paper that rested on a lightbox table. This lighted table allowed the cartoonist to see the drawings on the sheet of paper beneath the sheet he was drawing on. The first figure would be drawn on the first sheet of paper. Then the second figure, its position changed just a bit, would be drawn on the second sheet. This gave the impression that the figure was moving. It often took 45,000 drawings to make a six-and-a-half-minute cartoon.

Once all the drawings were made, they were traced onto transparent sheets of celluloid. The celluloid sheets were photographed one by one to make the film. It took 24 photographs to make one second of the cartoon.

When Fred Moore took over as Mickey's cartoonist, he gave Mickey a pear-shaped body. He also replaced Mickey's pencil-thin arms and legs with ones that were a little shorter and thicker. This is the shape we've come to recognize as Mickey Mouse.

These days, the creation of a cartoon is much more complicated than it was in the early 1900s. Making a cartoon involves many people—storymen, layout artists, and draftsmen. And

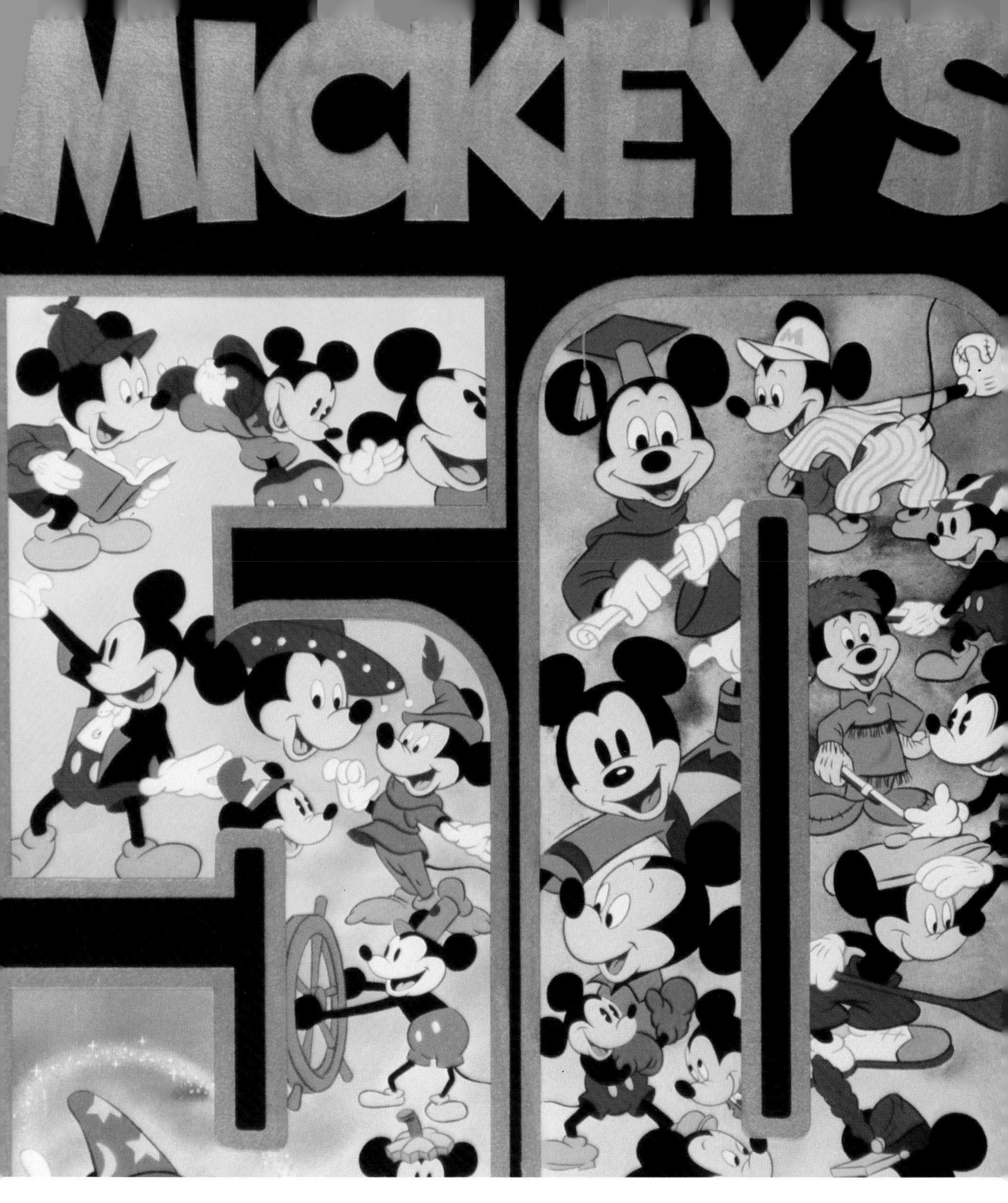

The many faces of Mickey Mouse—from his early days to the present.

their techniques and equipment are much more complex—the artists even use computers. It is fun and interesting to see just how far Mickey Mouse has come from the days when he was drawn by hand out of circles.

Mickey Gets an Oscar

Mickey Mouse appeared in over 70 black-and-white films from 1928 to 1935. Each cartoon cost between $25,000 and $40,000 to make, which was a lot of money in those days. In 1932, Walt Disney received an Oscar—Hollywood's highest award—for the creation of Mickey Mouse.

Then a new idea was added to the cartoons—color. Mickey's first color cartoon was titled *The Band Concert.* In the film, Mickey plays a bandleader who conducts an orchestra while battling a tornado. Donald Duck makes his first appearance. The film made Mickey the most popular star in Hollywood—and made Disney Studios the top animators.

Not only was Mickey Mouse popular in America, he now had fans everywhere in the world. Mickey Mouse Clubs were started in many countries, with over one million members. Goodyear Rubber Company made a 50-foot inflatable Mickey Mouse for the famous Macy's Thanksgiving Day Parade in 1935. Stores sold Mickey Mouse games, toys, books, and watches. Mickey was even given his own entry in the *Encyclopaedia Britannica.*

The Sorcerer's Apprentice

Though Mickey Mouse was a huge success, Disney was concerned that his star might lose his popularity. So he began looking for something new for Mickey. One night, while listening to classical music, Disney found what he was looking for. It was called *The Sorcerer's Apprentice.*

The symphony tells of a young man studying to be a magician in a sorcerer's castle. To make his chores easier, the young man uses one of his master's spells to bring a broomstick to life.

He commands the broomstick to fetch pails of water and dump them into a tub. The plan works well—until the young man realizes he cannot stop the broomstick from fetching more water. The young man takes an axe and cuts the broomstick. But each splinter becomes another broomstick that fetches more water. Soon the entire castle is overrun with pail-carrying broomsticks that flood the castle.

The story was perfect for the mischievious Mickey. *The Sorcerer's Apprentice* was made for an amazing $125,000. The film became part of *Fantasia*, a collection of classical music illustrated with Disney animation. Shown in 1940, *Fantasia* was called one of the best movies of its time. People everywhere agreed that Mickey Mouse was never better.

Mickey Mouse vs. Adolf Hitler

When America entered World War II in 1941, Disney used Mickey Mouse in training films. Mickey showed factory workers how to put rivets into planes and tanks. He asked people to buy war bonds so America could have more money to fight the war. One film, titled *All Together* (1942), showed Mickey and his friends cheering for America in a parade. The film did much to keep America's hopes high during the war.

Adolf Hitler, the German leader who started World War II, actually feared Mickey Mouse. He knew how popular Mickey was even in Germany. He was afraid the German people might become affected by Mickey's good nature. Hitler tried to keep Germany's movie theaters from playing Mickey Mouse cartoons. But the German people were so upset that Hitler decided to let Mickey back into the theaters.

Goodbye, Mickey Mouse?

After the war, Mickey appeared in eight short cartoons. *The Simple Things* (1953) was Mickey's last movie-theater appearance for 30 years. Disney was too busy working on plans for Disneyland in California to worry about Mickey's career. Somehow, he knew Mickey's popularity would never die.

Though Mickey Mouse seemed finished with movies, a new form of entertainment wanted him—television.

"The Mickey Mouse Club"

In 1955, ABC-TV broadcasted the first "Mickey Mouse Club" show. It ran five nights a week for four years. Over 12 million kids watched the show each night.

Disney auditioned thousands of children for the cast. Twenty-four were chosen to host the show. They were called *Mouseketeers*. They wore Mouseketeer hats (black hats with mouse ears). Some of the more famous names were Darlene, Bobby, Sharon, Karen, Cubby, Lonnie, and Annette (Funicello). Two adults, Jimmie and Roy, also helped to host the show. The show opened with the famous "Mickey Mouse

Members of the original
"Mickey Mouse Club."

March." *Who's the leader of the club that's made for you and me? M-I-C-K-E-Y M-O-U-S-E.* Then Mickey introduced the show's theme.

Monday was "Fun with Music Day." The Mouseketeers danced and sang for the audience. Tuesday was "Guest Star Day." Famous people—mostly Hollywood actors and actresses—participated in skits and activities. Wednesday was "Stunt Day" where anything could happen. Thursday was "Circus Day," and Mickey started the show in a bandleader's uniform. Friday was "Talent Roundup Day." The Mousketeers performed a variety of dances, songs, and skits. Everyday on the show there would be games, cartoons, music—even news.

The "Mickey Mouse Club" ran until 1959. Then its reruns were released, and the show was seen throughout the 1960s—even in France, Italy, Finland, Japan, Mexico, and Switzerland. The show can still be seen on the Disney Channel.

In 1977, a new "Mickey Mouse Club" was created. Twelve new Mousketeers performed a variety of entertainment to the sounds of rock music. And once again, Mickey Mouse was on hand—in a jumpsuit—to welcome viewers to the show.

Welcome to the Magic Kingdoms

In 1955, Disneyland in Aneheim, California, opened for business. Mickey Mouse was there to lead the first customers into the fantasy park.

The world has never seen anything like Disneyland. It has five theme parks. In Fantasyland, people enjoy the wonders of Sleeping Beauty Castle. In Adventureland, visitors take a thrilling journey through Africa on the Jungle Boat Ride. Frontierland takes us all back to a time in American history when life was simple and peaceful. MainStreet USA is the site for many of the exciting parades that are led by Mickey Mouse. And in Tomorrowland, there is the People Mover—an electric tram that helps people travel through the park.

Walt Disney looks over the plans
for Disneyland.

But there's a lot more to Disneyland. It has a futuristic monorail, roller coasters, a submarine ride, mechanical figures, street musicians, fireworks displays, a haunted house, and its own railroad and streetcars. Last but not least is the Mickey Mouse Review, a lively music show featuring a mechanical Mickey Mouse.

In 1971, Mickey was on hand to help open Walt Disney World in Orlando, Florida. Disney World is even more spectacular than Disneyland. It is 43 square miles and is filled with amazing rides, golf courses, a crystal palace, a submarine fleet, shopping centers, and a hotel. Many of the theme parks at Walt Disney World are the same as the ones at Disneyland, only much larger.

EPCOT Center also makes Walt Disney World much different than Disneyland. EPCOT stands for Experimental Prototype Community of Tomorrow. It is an amazing showcase for the world of the future. No one who goes to Walt Disney World should skip the wonders of EPCOT.

Disneyland and Disney World are not the only magical kingdoms created by Walt Disney. There's even a Tokyo Disneyland. It opened in 1983—and has many of the thrilling sites and rides of the other Disney theme parks. Mickey Mouse was there for the opening celebration—appearing in traditional Japanese dress.

Every year, millions of people from all over the world visit Disneyland, Disney World, and the Tokyo Disneyland. When they do, Mickey Mouse is there to welcome them to Disney's world of fun, excitement, and magic.

Fifty-Year-Old Mouse

In 1978, Mickey Mouse became the first cartoon character to have a gold star placed in his name on Hollywood Boulevard's famous Walk of Fame. It was part of a national celebration of Mickey's 50 birthday. NBC-TV held an hour-long birthday special. Mickey also appeared on the show "Saturday Night Live."

A poster celebrating Mickey's 50th birthday.

"Guess Who's Making A Comeback?"

In 1981, an amazing newspaper article appeared in the *Daily News* in Hollywood. "Guess who's making a comeback?" the article asked. "Mickey Mouse—that's who!"

It was true, and Mickey Mouse fans everywhere were delighted. The new movie was titled *Mickey's Christmas Carol.* It was based on Charles Dickens' famous book *A Christmas Carol.* Mickey played the role of Bob Cratchit, the overworked employee of Ebenezer Scrooge. The movie came out at Christmas time in 1983, and it was an instant hit.

Since then, Mickey's movie career has slowed again. These days, Mickey can be found at Disney World, Disneyland, and hosting the Disney Channel on cable television. One thing is certain—Mickey will always be around.

Mickey's Gang

Over the years, Mickey developed a group of "friends" who appeared with him in most of his cartoons. Some of these friends are Minnie Mouse, Donald Duck, Pluto, Goofy, Carolyn Cow, Patricia Pig, Clara Cluck the Hen, Robert the Rooster, and Henry Horse.

Donald Duck went on to become almost as popular as Mickey himself. He has his own cartoons and comic strip. Goofy and Pluto also became very popular. They were often featured together in their own cartoons.

Minnie Mouse became Mickey's closest friend. She was with him in his first cartoon, and appeared in most of Mickey's films afterwards. They were always romantically involved, and Mickey was usually saving her from some sort of trouble.

Did Mickey and Minnie ever get married? The wedding was never shown on the screen, but Walt Disney did confess that the marriage might

Mickey enjoys a happy moment
with his friends.

have taken place. "In private life," he said, "Mickey is married to Minnie. What it really amounts to is that Minnie is, for screen purposes, his leading lady."

Some of Mickey's foes include Pegleg Pete, Hound Dog, and Claws the Cat. Pegleg Pete—a big, mean cat who is missing one leg—is the most famous of these foes. He appeared in many of Mickey's first cartoons, including *Steamboat Willie.*

"See You Real Soon!"

So now we've returned to the question asked at the beginning of the book: What has made Mickey Mouse the most famous cartoon character in the world? The answer is simple: Mickey *is* funny, his *stories* are funny—and he has become a friend and hero to kids and adults everywhere.

"See you real soon!"